Rain
ANIM

Flame Fights Back

Rainbow
ANIMAL HOSPITAL

Flame Fights Back

Steve Attridge

Collins
An imprint of HarperCollinsPublishers

Rainbow
ANIMAL HOSPITAL

by Steve Attridge

Bartholomew the Champion
Trash Cat's Secret
Toffee's Big Problem
Thumper the Brave
Mango's Great Escape

For my son, Jacob.
Also, thanks to Ailsa McIntosh and all staff at
M.M. Leggett veterinary practise, for their help.
Any factual errors remain mine alone.

First published in Great Britain by Collins in 1998
Collins is an imprint of HarperCollins*Publishers* Ltd
77-85 Fulham Palace Road, Hammersmith, London, W6 8JB

1 3 5 7 9 8 6 4 2

Text copyright © Steve Attridge 1998
Illustrations © John Bennett 1998

ISBN 0 00 675360-4

The author asserts the moral right
to be identified as the author of the work.

Printed and bound in Great Britain by
Caledonian International Book Manufacturing Ltd,
Glasgow G64

Chapter One
AN EMERGENCY

The car bumped along the muddy track, brambles scratching its side. Hilary David, one of the vets from the Rainbow Animal Hospital, sat hunched over the steering wheel, her knuckles white from gripping it so tightly. Beside her was Eddie Wright, watching the track ahead with as much concentration as Hilary. The car, a battered Fiat Panda, gave a violent lurch as it hit a rock and Eddie fell against the door. He tightened his seat belt. He hoped they would be in time.

He could tell from the tight lines on Hilary's face that she had her doubts. And if they were too late, what would they find? What would have happened? Farmer Draper had said that she might make it. She might not.

They turned a bend and there, about a quarter of a mile ahead, was Meadow Farm. Hilary put her foot down and the car lurched faster.

"Proper little Damon Hill, aren't you?" said Eddie. "You have only two speeds – fast and very fast."

Eddie knew he could cheek Hilary because she wasn't even listening. She turned briefly to him and said, "I know you want to watch, but I may need you to help too. If I ask you to do something, just do it. No questions. Right?"

"Right," said Eddie.

Hilary meant business.

The farm was a shambles. All the fencing and gates were broken, and rusting machinery was lying around. Farmer Draper had the reputation for being a bit of a skinflint and, judging by the look of the farm, he hadn't spent much on its upkeep for some time. As the car screeched to a halt, he came out of a barn. He was a large man with pork-chop whiskers and a battered trilby hat that looked as if he never took it off, even when he went to bed. He was wearing a dirty old apron which

was smeared with blood. He was wiping his hands on a cloth.

"So much for hygiene," Hilary hissed between her teeth. "Come on, Eddie. Action stations!"

The three of them trudged through the mud to the barn. From inside came a whinny and a puffing sound that meant someone was in great pain.

It was cold in the barn. A single light bulb hung from a wire, providing a small shaft of light. The rest was in shadow and the place smelled of ancient hay, muck and cows. Lying on her side under the weak pool of light was a large chestnut horse, her belly swollen, in labour. Her coat was damp and sweating, and steam was rising from it. The eye Eddie saw was large and wild – the eye of panic. She tried to move, but the effort was immense and the pain greater – her whinnying sounded like a scream. Two cows were looking over from an adjacent stall. Both chewed occasionally, but were too engrossed in watching Bess to do anything else. Eddie wanted to look away but he made himself face the great horse. She might need him.

Hilary approached slowly and let the horse get a good look at her face. She stroked Bess's flanks soothingly, then her muzzle, cooing and whispering to her: "Good girl, there we go, good Bess."

She turned to Farmer Draper.

"How long has she been in labour?" she asked.

"Oh, I reckon . . . about five hours," he said, tilting his hat back on his head to reveal a great bald dome, pink and smooth as a baby's.

"Then why didn't you call me before? She's in a lot of pain!" said Hilary, barely concealing the anger she felt.

"Didn't know she was that bad. I can't be calling out the vet every five minutes, not at forty quid a throw."

Hilary decided it was best to say nothing more. Besides, she didn't have time to argue – she was going to be too busy. Bess had lost a lot of blood and was in a great deal of pain. Hilary opened her bag and took out a syringe. She measured out some painkiller – enough to help but not too much or Bess might become unconscious and therefore unable to help with the birth of her foal. Hilary injected Bess, then turned to Eddie.

"What I want you to do is comfort her. I need to find out what's going wrong and the more relaxed Bess is the better. OK?"

"Right," said Eddie.

He knelt beside Bess's great head and looked at the foam and mucus on the hay, the wet mouth and the wild eye. He stroked her muzzle and made small 'shhhhhh' noises. The eye looked at him from a long way off, then rolled back again into Bess's pain.

"Is he qualified? Looks too young to me," said Farmer Draper.

"You don't need to be qualified to comfort an animal," said Hilary. "Of course, you could always do it, if you prefer."

"He'll do, I suppose," said Farmer Draper.

Eddie continued to stroke Bess, aware of the large moony eyes of the cows behind him. The painkiller had taken hold a little, but only to ease, not eradicate the pain. Bess was taking small, exhausted breaths. She could not keep it up for much longer. The foal was caught sideways inside her, which meant that it could not be born properly.

"The foal is breached, Mr Draper. Stuck fast. I can feel it. I'm not sure that I can save it," said Hilary, looking up at the farmer.

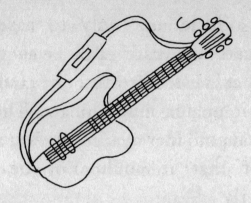

Chapter Two

THE END AND THE BEGINNING

Greg had got carried away. Chelsea had said that she would like a big expensive engagement party with a string quartet playing, and Greg had said if that's what she wanted, then that's what she would get. What about the cost? she wanted to know. No problem, he assured her. He had some money put away for a rainy day and that would easily be enough.

What he didn't tell her was exactly how much he had put away: thirteen pounds and forty pence. He had already done a few calculations for the party and the cheapest he thought he could get away with was about a hundred pounds for food and drink, another thirty or forty to hire a room and, horror of horrors, after a few phone calls, the cheapest he could hire a string quartet for was a hundred and fifty pounds. Greg was a heavy metal man at heart and it cut him deeply to think of paying all that money just to listen to some boring classical music. That was nearly three hundred pounds altogether. His heart sank lower than his bank balance.

*

It was surgery time and Chelsea sat at the reception desk. The hospital was busy: there were two cats, one with a cough and the other with mange; four dogs, one with toothache, one with a cut paw and two for booster injections; and a rabbit with an eye infection. There was also a man sitting with a large covered bird cage.

Greg approached and Chelsea smiled in a way that always made Eddie feel slightly sick. Her 'cheese and chocolate smile' he called it.

"Greg, during lunch I was wondering, do you think we could have everyone at the party in formal evening dress? We could all hire suits and gowns and it would go with the string quartet. What do you think?"

What Greg thought rated an 'X' certificate, but what he said was:

"What? Oh, sure. No problem. Dicky bows and posh frocks it is.

"Are you sure you have enough?" she asked.

"Yeah. 'Course I have. Tons of money," he lied.

"We can use my savings too," said Chelsea.

"No, I insist. I said I'd pay for the lot and that's what I'm going to do," Greg said, wondering where on earth he was going to find the money.

"I can just see our Eddie in an evening suit, can't you?" she said.

"Not really," said Greg. "Where *is* Eddie anyway?"

"On an emergency call out. He's been pestering Hilary for some time and she promised he could go on the next one. It's his half term."

*

At Meadow Farm Bess was having a worse time than before. Hilary had managed to reach inside her and manoeuvre the foal's legs under its little body, but now the baby was in danger of suffocating. Bess had lost more blood and Hilary began to fear the worst. She turned to the farmer.

"Mr Draper, I'm afraid you'll have to make a decision. Either the mother or the baby. I'm not sure that I can save them both," she said.

Eddie felt the hot damp head of the horse and looked up at Farmer Draper. He scratched his head and pulled his hat down onto his forehead.

"Why's it always me, eh? Why can't it have been an easy one?" he asked bitterly.

"With all due respect, it's the horse which is suffering," Hilary said.

"You try runnin' a bloomin' farm," Draper said.

He looked at Bess. Eddie wondered if he was already calculating how much he would get for Bess's body if she died, and offsetting this against the cost of another horse.

"Which has most chance, mother or littl'un?" he asked.

"Very difficult to say," said Hilary.

Farmer Draper looked at Bess again, then back at Hilary.

"Get the young'un born if you can. Maybe old Bess'll come through too."

Eddie held Bess's head and whispered gently in her ear, though sometimes her pain put her beyond listening. Hilary tried to turn the foal around again. It seemed to take an age. Then Bess gave a loud whinny that broke Eddie's heart and with a powerful WHOOSH, which took them all by surprise, skinny, stalky legs appeared, then a bewildered and wet head, and the foal was there.

Hilary sat back for a second, exhausted, then set about making sure the foal took deep breaths to get its lungs working. She was worried that all the time it had been stuck in its mother without oxygen may have caused some damage. Eddie turned back to Bess.

"Well done, girl. Clever girl," he said. But he was too late. Bess was dead.

Chapter Three

A NEW PATIENT

Before they left, Hilary arranged to go back to Meadow Farm later that day because the foal would now have to be hand reared and that would take planning, time and effort.

"Don't be too hard on him," said Hilary, as she and Eddie drove back to the Rainbow Animal Hospital.

Eddie felt cut to the quick at the death of Bess, but also angry that Farmer Draper hadn't shown much emotion.

"Some farmers are like that. It's a hard life and they just don't get sentimental about animals. They can't afford to," she explained

"Then they shouldn't be allowed to have them," said Eddie.

"You like hamburgers and bacon, don't you? How would you feel about working in an abattoir and killing your own food?" said Hilary.

It was a harsh thing to say, but she was right. Eddie liked Hilary because she treated him as an adult, even if she did say things that made you feel a bit wobbly sometimes. Eddie was going to say something about *that* being different, but the words died in his throat. Hilary might be right, but he still didn't like Draper, or the way he had looked at the new-born foal, as if somehow it was the foal's fault that her mother had died.

When they arrived back at the animal hospital Hilary was immediately in action, setting the broken leg of a dog whom Ron had just bought in from a nasty road accident. Eddie went to help Chelsea, who was trying to deal with several people at once. From the small consulting room behind her came a terrible commotion, as if someone was being strangled: "Help! Help! Man overboard! Man overboard! Bring out the harpoons!"

"Who's that?" asked Eddie.

"Go and see for yourself. And try to get him to shut up," Chelsea said.

Eddie entered the consulting room and looked around. He was surprised because, despite the racket coming from the room moments before, it was now empty. Or was it? On the table was a cage and in the cage was a beautiful parrot. The bird put its head on one side and eyed Eddie suspiciously with one glittering black eye.

"Hello," said Eddie.

The parrot listened but carried on looking silently. It had wonderful green and red tail feathers and a green chest. Around its cheeks was yellow. Eddie noticed that one wing was tucked in at an odd angle, so he assumed it had been damaged and that was why the bird was here.

"Cat got your tongue?" asked Eddie.

The bird opened its beak as if it was about to speak, then closed it again.

Eddie turned to go, but as he reached the door a voice said: "Spanish doubloons! Yo ho ho and a bottle of coke!"

Eddie turned quickly but the bird looked at him defiantly, its beak closed. Eddie turned his back and the bird spoke again.

"Man overboard!"

Eddie turned again and the bird was silent.

"So, bit of a joker, are you?" Eddie asked.

The bird turned and lifted its tail feathers at him. Eddie smiled and went back to help Chelsea. This bird, whatever his name was, was going to be a lot of fun.

After helping Chelsea, Eddie went to the rest room. Greg was sitting hunched over a notebook, scribbling something.

"Writing your memoirs?" asked Eddie.

"You could call it *The Life and Times of a Great Div*."

Greg didn't even hear, let alone respond.

"What's up?" asked Eddie.

"What? Oh, nothing," lied Greg, who was desperately trying to work out how much money he'd get if he sold a few things; like his bicycle and record collection.

He'd promised Chelsea a grand engagement party and now he'd dug that hole for himself he'd have to find a way out.

Eddie spent the rest of the afternoon cleaning the wards. He also found out from Kalim, one of the nurses, that the parrot was called Nelson. He had got injured when his owner had let him out; he was flying around the living room when he got stuck behind the curtain rail and panicked, damaging his wing. His owner had been in the Navy, which was why Nelson tended to talk only about nautical things.

Just as Eddie was about to leave the hospital for the day, Hilary came into Reception, slamming the doors so hard that they rattled in their hinges. Clearly something had angered her and Eddie wasn't going to leave until he found out what it was.

Chapter Four

A PLAN FORMS

Hilary stormed into the office of the chief vet, Mr Wensleydale, or Old Cheesy, as Eddie called him. Eddie listened outside the door as he and Hilary discussed Farmer Draper. She had been back to see him as they had agreed, but now he was refusing to pay the bill.

"He had the cheek to say 'vetting wasn't proper women's work'," said Hilary.

"But presumably that isn't the reason he refuses to pay," said Old Cheesy.

"No. He objected to Eddie being there. Said that using kids as nurses was doing things on the cheap, and illegal too," said Hilary.

"Did Eddie actually assist?" asked Old Cheesy.

"He helped to calm Bess. He was extremely good, as he usually is with animals," said Hilary.

"But the point is, if he made an official complaint, it could look bad for us," said Old Cheesy.

Outside, Eddie thought it was typical of Old Cheesebreath to take someone else's point of view, especially if it was against Eddie.

"So you think we should just leave it?" asked Hilary.

"Yes."

"But what about the foal?"

"What about it?"

"Draper says he can't afford the time or money to 'nursemaid' a foal, so he wants to sell her," said Hilary.

"She belongs to him. If he wants to sell her, that's his business," said Old Cheesy.

"But she needs a great deal of care and attention at the moment. It might be difficult to find a buyer who'll do that."

Outside, Eddie listened to them until he realised it was one of those conversations that would just go round and round in circles, so he left and went home.

*

That evening Eddie sat in his bedroom idly playing with his Game Boy, but not really concentrating. He was playing Tetris and could normally easily get up to sixty or seventy lines, but tonight his mind wasn't on it and the lines of bricks kept building up until he lost and had to start again. His little sister Kate had been in the room looking at him for several minutes before Eddie even realised she was there.

"So what's up with you then?" she asked.

Eddie frowned. He might as well tell her because if Kate wanted to know something, you kept it from her at your peril. She could make life difficult for anyone if she chose to. Eddie told her about the foal and what Farmer Draper intended to do.

"He can't," said Kate.

"How are we going to stop him?" asked Eddie.

"Threats, persuasion, blackmail, violence. There's loads of ways to make someone do something, or not do something," said Kate.

Not for the first time in his life, Eddie marvelled at the radical difference between Kate's sweet looks and the coils of snakes that sometimes writhed inside her head. When she had been only five years old she had kept a secret book of imaginary tortures and it was the most disgusting thing Eddie had ever sneaked a look at.

Kate walked up and down the room for a few minutes, turning on her heels when she reached the wall. Then she faced Eddie.

"It's dead easy," she said.

"What are you talking about?" asked Eddie.

"The problem is there's this baby pony that needs a lot of looking after, and Farmer Draper won't do it. Right?"

"Right," said Eddie.

"So *we* do it," said Kate. "And 'cos we're doing it for free he can't complain."

"But . . ." began Eddie, then he realised that it was rather a good idea.

There were details that needed working out, such as the fact that the foal needed someone with her twenty-four hours a day for a time, but Kate suggested a shift system with other children – two at a time, plus a few older kids for the night shift. There was also the problem of Old Cheesy, who had already criticised Eddie's presence at the farm. Kate suggested that what he didn't know wouldn't hurt him. They, and their friends, would keep it to themselves.

"So – are you up for it?" asked Kate.

"Yeah. Let's do it!" said Eddie.

Chapter Five

THE DIFFICULT PATIENT

Eddie wanted to spend the next morning at the hospital, so Kate agreed to round up some other children and meet him at Meadow Farm later. At the hospital Nelson was proving to be a demanding patient. Sometimes he stood on the bottom of his cage with his head drooping against his damaged wing feeling very sorry for himself, occasionally muttering 'Poor Polly, poor Polly'. At other times he got in a rage and spat seed at anyone who happened to be passing his cage. Or he would suddenly scream at the top of his voice 'Man overboard! Man overboard! To the lifeboats! Ha ha ha! Yo ho ho!'

Most of the staff didn't mind, but there was something about the parrot's shrieking tone that jangled Mr Wensleydale's nerves to barbed wire. He felt constantly on edge and it was no better when Nelson was quiet, because Mr Wensleydale sat in his office waiting for the shriek to echo down the corridor from the ward. What was worse was the fact that Nelson's owner had gone abroad for a month, so the parrot would be at the hospital even *after* his wing had healed.

Eddie stood looking at Nelson. Nelson stood on his perch looking back at Eddie. It was a competition – who would look away first? Eddie kept staring until his eyes felt salty and stinging, then he blinked.

"All right, you win this time," he said.

Nelson shrieked with laughter, and Eddie heard the sound of Mr Wensleydale slamming his door. At that moment an idea popped into Eddie's head that was just too delicious to resist. It would take a bit of time, but it would be worth it.

An hour later Eddie cycled to Meadow Farm to meet Kate. She was in the lane leading to the farm and had obviously done a good morning's work. Eddie's best mate Imran was there, and two

other girls, Ailsa and Aruna. Kate had also got a promise from Imran's big brother, Prakash, that either he or one of his friends, all of whom were eighteen or more, would help on night duty until the foal was weaned. Kalim from the animal hospital had agreed to meet them at the farm to show them how to look after the foal.

They wheeled their bikes along the lane. It was muddy and full of cow pats. Imran looked in distaste at the wheels of his bike, caked with stuff that he didn't even like to think about, let alone have to wash off when he got home.

"I hate the countryside," he said.

"It's all right, just stinks a bit," said Kate.

"But there's no shops or McDonalds or nothing," said Imran. "And there's all them wild animals."

"What wild animals, you divvy?" asked Eddie.

"I dunno. Bulls and chickens and stuff," said Imran.

"Chickens! Oh sure. Giant chickens that jump out of trees and peck you to death," said Eddie.

They arrived at the farm. Farmer Draper was hauling some new fencing from his beaten-up old truck. his sleeves were rolled up and he was sweating. He looked at the group of children.

"Hello. I was here the other day when ... when Bess died," said Eddie.

Farmer Draper looked at him and said nothing. He clearly wasn't going to make this easy.

"You know you were thinking of selling the foal?" said Eddie.

Farmer Draper said nothing, so he

continued.

"Well, we thought that if we looked after it until it's weaned. For free. Then maybe you might keep her. I mean, she'd be worth a lot more and it wouldn't cost you anything for us to look after her," said Eddie.

Farmer Draper stared.

"There's no law against answering," said Kate.

Eddie wanted to boot her but didn't. She might boot him back even harder. Farmer Draper didn't even hear her. He was thinking. A foal that needed weaning was a lot of work and if this lot were prepared to do it, then he could still sell her afterwards if he wanted to. He might keep her if she quietened down, but he had a feeling that she was going to be a nervy, frisky one. A lot of hard work. While he was having his big think

Kalim arrived. Farmer Draper looked at her, then at the children.

"You're on. You can sleep in the barn with the foal, but I want notes from your parents to say they agree. I don't want no complaints nor trouble. She's in the barn over there, feeding stuff's on the shelf, milk's in the churn. Let her out in the paddock for a while," he said, and went back to work.

The children looked at each other, then leaned their bikes against the barn and went inside, followed by Kalim.

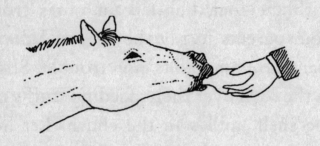

Chapter Six
A Christening

The foal was standing in a stall on its stick-like legs. It looked at the children, as they entered, with its large limpid eyes.

"Hello, girl," said Eddie, approaching slowly with his hand out. The foal backed away a little, then snorted.

Eddie waited, then the foal allowed him to stroke her muzzle.

"Ah, look at her," said Ailsa.

"She's a beaut'," said Kate.

"Not very big, is she?" said Imran, never one to ignore the obvious.

"Well, she's a baby, she's not meant to be," said Aruna.

The foal had a reddish-brown coat. A streak of sunlight shone on the red and made it a dazzling burnt-copper colour. Kalim told the children how often she should be fed, and showed them the correct amount to give her. They measured out some milk and Imran held out the bottle to the foal, who sniffed and nuzzled it, then took it in her mouth and tossed it aside.

"Hold it tighter!" said Aruna.

Eventually the foal had a good feed, then they tried to put a rope around her neck to lead her outside. She backed away, tossed her head, and obviously didn't like the idea. Eddie whispered quietly to her, then stroked her mane while he slipped the rope gently around her neck and led her outside. As they entered the yard she blinked in the sunlight and looked around curiously. She walked a bit unsteadily, but with great determination. In the paddock she took a few tottering steps and flicked her tail, then did a little hop and almost fell, her legs splaying, but she righted herself and snorted. Eddie could see already that here was a little pony with a lot of spirit and a big personality. Only one day old, all alone, but not beaten.

The sun streaked her coat a golden red.

"Ace coat!" said Ailsa.

"What's her name?" asked Imran.

"Hasn't got one," said Eddie.

"She's got to have a name," said Aruna.

"I know," said Kate.

They all looked at her.

"Flame," said Kate. "Because of her colouring, and because there's something bright and lively about her."

It was a good name.

Kate dipped her hand in the water trough and approached the little foal. She dabbed a few drops of water on her nose.

"I name you . . . Flame!" she said.

Flame lifted her head and tried to whinny like a big pony would. Then she scuffed the ground with a front hoof.

"See? She likes it!" said Kate.

*

They spent another half hour outside, then took Flame back to her stall, where she settled down in the straw for a sleep.

The children left the farm and Eddie went to the hospital where he had something important to do, something secret. Then he went home and packed for what was going to be a long night. At eight o'clock Eddie's dad drove him to the farm. Imran and his big brother, Prakash, were already there. Farmer Draper showed them the place in the barn where they could sleep. They had an adult with them and Imran had his dad's mobile phone to call home in an emergency.

They fed Flame again and made a fuss of her, then climbed up to the loft where there was a big pile of hay. They had blankets and sleeping bags and

enough food for an army. Eddie had a large flask of hot chocolate and they sat talking until everything around them grew dark and quiet. They arranged to take it in turns to feed Flame every few hours and Eddie set the alarm on his digital watch that Chelsea had bought him for his birthday. Soon Imran was snoring like a pair of bagpipes and Eddie lay thinking how strange it was to be there. The thing about working with animals was you never knew where it would lead you.

Chapter Seven

A RUDE AWAKENING

The night in the barn was brilliant, as far as Eddie was concerned. He lay there for a while wondering if there were rats or spiders in the hay, watching and waiting from secret places, how big they might be and what they might do to him when he fell asleep, then he got fed up with being frightened and became interested in the strange quality of Imran's snores, which now sounded like a hoover backfiring. Then he dozed off, as Imran's brother listened to his Walkman.

Eddie was woken up three hours later by his alarm. He shivered slightly as he got out of his sleeping bag. Farmer Draper had left the light on, although he complained about how much it would cost. Eddie climbed down and went to Flame, who looked up at him with her large, curious eyes.

"Hello, Flame," he said, as he prepared a bottle for her, then lay on the straw beside her as she fed.

She had a wonderful clean smell and her coat was glossy, as if freshly shampooed. She should be snuggled up with her mother thought Eddie and he wondered if she felt lonely. He lay back on the straw and stroked Flame's head. His eyes felt heavy and it was warm beside the little foal. Soon there was just the darkness and a dream in which Flame was older and running like the wind across a field. Sitting on her was Nelson the parrot who was screeching happily and shouting 'You can't catch me now! Not on this little beauty!'

During the next week everyone kept to the rota and Eddie couldn't wait until it was his turn again to spend the night at the farm. Already Flame had grown bigger and was getting stronger.

One morning, as he sat by Flame, almost dozing off, Eddie was roused by voices. He opened his eyes and Farmer Draper and another man were looking down at him and Flame. Flame struggled to her feet. Eddie didn't like

the way the man was looking at her, as if he was sizing up something in a butcher's shop.

"Nice looking little filly," said the man.

"Won't find better," said Farmer Draper.

"Who's he?" said another, younger voice.

Eddie looked, and standing by the door was a girl of about fifteen, dressed in smart green jodhpurs and a hacking jacket. She looked very posh. The man was called Dicky Raban and she was his daughter.

"Boy's helping to wean her," said Farmer Draper.

The girl approached, brushed past Eddie and peered at Flame. She held out her hand and Flame nipped it – not hard, but enough to make the girl know she shouldn't take liberties without permission.

"Ouch!" said the girl.

Dicky Raban laughed.

"Take it easy with her, Sam. She's only a baby," he said, turning to Farmer Draper. "She's got character. How much did you say?"

"Eight hundred," said the farmer. "This is a quality pony."

"But it's having to be hand reared. Might have a few rough edges that need knocking off. Six fifty," said Dicky.

"Done," said Draper.

Dicky smiled at his daughter.

"You've got yourself a pony, my love," he said.

"Good. Can we go now? I'm freezing," said Sam, turning on her heels and trudging towards a blue Mercedes.

"I'll send a cheque. We'll collect her in, say, three weeks. She should be OK to move then," said Dicky.

Eddie had slowly come to his senses and stood listening, almost in a state of shock. He couldn't believe it. Farmer Draper had just sold Flame. She was so little. And that Sam girl was a spoilt brat. It wasn't right. He watched as Dicky Raban followed his daughter into the car and the Mercedes skidded out of the yard, spraying mud back at the barn.

"You can't do it," said Eddie to Farmer Draper. "I won't let you do it!"

Chapter Eight

HOW TO SAVE FLAME?

"You can't sell Flame just like that. She's still a baby, and her mother has died," said Eddie.

"She's *my* pony and I can do what I like," said Farmer Draper. "And if you don't like it you can push off."

He turned on his heels and left.

Eddie bent down and nuzzled against Flame. She got to her feet and he took her outside. She seemed to be getting stronger so quickly. A sleepy Imran and his brother joined them. Eddie told his friends what had happened.

"That's it, then. Might as well go home," said Imran.

"No, that is *not* it. We're going to keep coming to the farm, and we're going to find a way to save Flame. You should've seen the girl whose dad wants to buy her. She's a right little madam," said Eddie.

"Why don't we just give up? It's easier," said Imran.

"That's my little brother for you," said Prakash. "His motto is 'If at first you don't succeed, give up and go home'. Mr Motivator you are not."

"I'm just being realistic," said Imran.

But Eddie wasn't listening. Already a plan was forming in his mind and he needed time to refine the details.

Greg's plans also needed refining. He had sold his record collection, his electric guitar, a set of weights he had bought but used only once because it hurt to lift them, a few magazine collections and an old typewriter. That had come to two hundred and fifty pounds, but he was still over a hundred short for the party and hiring their outfits. He thought of applying for a bank loan but getting in debt was no way out. He would just have to go through his things again and see what else he could sell. The party was meant to be in a month's time and he knew Chelsea thought he had everything in hand. How had he got himself into this situation?

Greg was deep in thought when Eddie came in. He fed the hospital dogs, Emma and Hannibal, then sat down and sighed. Greg sat and sighed too.

"It's not fair," said Eddie.

"Too right," said Greg. "Nothing ever is."

Eddie told Greg about Flame and also decided to try out his great idea on him.

"See, what I thought is – we could buy her ourselves," said Eddie.

"We? Who's we?" asked Greg.

"Me, Kate, other kids. We could raise some money, then buy Flame ourselves."

"Just a few problems there," said Greg. "Where are you going to get six hundred and fifty quid? Where will you keep Flame even if you could buy her? How are you going to afford to keep and feed her even if you do the rest? Forget it, Eds."

"I just hate that. You come up with an idea and all people can do is think of a few minor problems," said Eddie, and he left Greg to go and spend some time with Nelson.

Emma trotted after him. In fact, she was the only one, apart from Eddie, who knew exactly why he was spending so much time with Nelson.

That evening Eddie shared his idea with Kate. She was much more enthusiastic.

"I like it. Positive thinking, Eds. Didn't think you had it in you," she said, already pacing up and down, her brow furrowed in thought.

Eddie sat on the bed and let her think.

Suddenly she stopped and turned to look at him.

"First things first. Raising dosh. We organise a garage sale, a car boot sale, the lot. We put out the word – everyone to donate stuff to sell. I'm talking quality goods here: CDs; computer games; sports equipment; videos; board games. Quality goods. No rubbish. We all have to make a sacrifice. We could also have a raffle and ask around local businesses – if they think they'll get a bit of good publicity they might cough up a few quid."

Kate's brain was in overdrive. This was how Eddie loved her: ideas spitting out of her like bullets. It made him think that with a lot of work and a bit of luck, they might just save Flame. Six hundred and fifty pounds was megabucks, but who could tell? And if they couldn't do it, it wouldn't be for want of trying.

Chapter Nine

INTO ACTION!

Kate designed some posters on the school computer and then distributed them at break and lunch time, until one of the teachers read one and made her re-design it. The poster said:

SAVE FLAME!

FLAME IS AN ORPHAN PONY
WHO IS BEING SOLD TO A
DINKHEAD UNLESS WE SAVE HER.

THIS MEANS YOU! YES, YOU!!!
SO STOP READING THIS AND
DONATE SOMETHING TO
KATE WRIGHT, CLASS 4G.
FAILURE TO COMPLY WILL LEAD
TO EXTREME VIOLENCE.
I KNOW WHERE YOU ALL LIVE
SO YOU WON'T BE SAFE
ANYWHERE!

SAVE FLAME!

Soon children started to bring things to Kate. Eddie also told his friends to pass on the word. Much to Mr Wensleydale's annoyance, Hilary let Eddie use a storeroom at the hospital as a dumping ground for things to sell. Every evening Eddie and Kate would arrive with bin liners and cardboard boxes full of items which they sorted into three piles: rubbish and tat; OK stuff; and the most important pile, which Kate called 'good little earners'.

Word soon got round, and children started to bring things to the hospital, too. Emma would help them sort it all out by dragging the bin liners around until they split, or jumping on the cardboard boxes. One evening while Eddie and Kate were going through the latest batch of stuff they could hear Mr Wensleydale and Hilary arguing next door:

MR WENSLEYDALE This is an animal hospital, not a jumble sale.

HILARY   The 'jumble' is for the benefit of an animal, as I keep telling you.

MR WENSLEYDALE Are you sure it isn't for the benefit of one Eddie Wright?

HILARY   What do you mean?

MR WENSLEYDALE   I mean that wherever I turn Eddie Wright seems to have a hand in things.

HILARY   I think you're over reacting.

MR WENSLEYDALE   I am merely pointing out that there are many occasions when Eddie Wright is a bothersome little tyke, an irksome *bête noire*.

"What's an 'ergsum bentoir'?" asked Kate.

"Search me, but Old Cheesy will be

sorry he said it," said Eddie, with a look on his face that made Kate wonder what he was up to.

Amongst the things brought in to sell was a perfectly good Sony Walkman, two hairdryers, a Game Boy and two watches. Eddie decided to take them to a second-hand electrical shop on his way home. As he entered the shop Greg was coming out, counting out a few five-pound notes.

"Greg! You selling stuff too?" asked Eddie.

Greg seemed embarrassed.

"What? No, no. Not me," said Greg.

"Then why are you counting that money?" asked Eddie.

Greg sighed. "OK, yes, I've just sold my camera. But . . ." he hesitated, "I'd rather you didn't tell Chelsea."

"Why not?"

"I just would," said Greg. "I mean, it is for a good cause and I just don't want her to think . . ." He trailed off, embarrassed.

Eddie assumed that Greg meant he would be embarrassed for Chelsea to know he was selling personal belongings to contribute to the Save Flame fund.

"Look, Greg, it's really cool that you're doing this," said Eddie.

"Do you think so? Really?" asked Greg.

"Sure. We all appreciate it," said Eddie.

"Right. Well, thanks Eds," said Greg, surprised at Eddie's reaction, or even that Eddie *knew* what he was selling the camera for.

He assumed that Chelsea had talked about the party and Eddie had worked

out for himself that it was going to be expensive. Greg left, taking with him an entirely different understanding than Eddie, of the conversation they had just shared.

At the weekend Eddie and Kate held a garage sale at their home. It was well attended and they sold over half the things. Their dad also took them to a Sunday morning car boot sale and they set up their own table. They sold everything else except a broken Darth Vader that Imran had donated. Despite this they had only twelve days to go before Flame was being sold. So far they had raised two hundred and eighty six pounds, which was phenomenal, but not nearly enough. The situation was starting to get desperate.

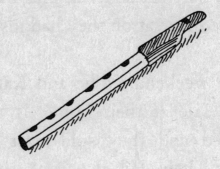

Chapter Ten

ANOTHER GOOD IDEA

Kate couldn't wait for it to finish. Orchestra practise. One of her few mistakes had been to express enthusiasm about joining the school orchestra. What she had in mind was a large kettle drum which she could whack to her heart's content, whatever anyone else

was doing. It wasn't music which interested her, more the idea of hitting something. What she got was a tin whistle that she still couldn't play and a threat of being grounded if she didn't attend rehearsals for at least a term.

She sat there listening to the string section doing all their fancy trills and runs, led by the dreaded Deidre Weatherburrow. After the rehearsal Kate skipped out as quickly as she could, but the dreaded Deidre's mother insisted on giving Kate a lift home, as she'd wrecked her bike and 'little girls shouldn't be out on their own'.

Kate sat in the back of the car not listening to Deidre prattle on about the orchestra, about eating sushi (whatever that was), the importance of maintaining correct posture and the need to appreciate the countryside. Apparently

Deidre believed in long walks and collecting wild flowers.

"What do you do at the weekend?" she asked Kate.

"What? Me? Oh, I just sort of hang out and try to avoid being seen with anoraks and nerds," said Kate.

"I often go to the Country Park," said Deidre.

"Amazing," said Kate sarcastically. "What do you do there – talk to the fairies?"

"No. Mostly look at the animals on the animal farm. They've got this wonderful place called Guinea-Pig Land, with little shops and everything. And there's the ponies, of course."

"What, they live there?" asked Kate, now interested.

"Yes. They have a great time. Everyone loves them."

A solution concerning just where Flame could be kept started to form in Kate's mind. Deidre might be a dipwit of the highest order, but she had given Kate a good idea. As soon as Kate got home she went to the telephone. She had some important calls to make.

Eddie and Imran watched as Flame walked and almost skipped around the paddock. She was getting stronger each day and seemed to look forward to Eddie being with her. She would nuzzle him and let him rest his head against her neck. Hilary had visited several times and pronounced Flame fit and healthy. Eddie had decided that it might be best if *she* asked Farmer Draper about the possibility of selling Flame to someone other than Dicky.

"Why should I? It's a firm offer. He's

already sent a cheque," said Draper.

"I'm just saying if another offer were made, would you consider it?" asked Hilary.

"Doubt it," said Draper.

"Flame is still very young. She might benefit from staying here longer, in a place with people she knows," said Hilary.

"Aye, and with a little pink bedroom of her own and a maid to bring in little cakes on a silver tray," said Draper.

"You're not very good at sarcasm, Mr Draper," said Hilary.

"And you're not very good at making me change my mind. Next Saturday she goes, whether you like it or not, missy."

It seemed hopeless. It was Eddie's turn to stay at the farm and as he, Imran and Prakash settled down he felt heavy-hearted. He had grown very fond of little Flame and felt that it would somehow be his fault if she ended up with the awful Sam girl. Eddie didn't trust her and what happened the next morning confirmed his worst fears.

Imran and Prakash had gone home for breakfast and Eddie was just packing up his sleeping bag and chatting to Flame when the Mercedes pulled into the yard. While her father talked to Farmer Draper, Sam entered the barn.

"Still nurse-maiding?" she asked.

"You got a problem with that?" asked Eddie.

"No. I just like to know who's hanging around my pony," she said, approaching Flame.

Sam took a carrot from her pocket and offered it to Flame. She sniffed it, looked suspiciously at Sam, then opened her mouth to take it. Sam withdrew her hand, offered the carrot again, then pulled it back. Flame snorted in annoyance.

"Give it to her!" said Eddie.

"No! She needs to learn who's boss. Ponies need strong discipline when they're young."

"That's not discipline, it's just teasing. It's just you showing what a drongohead you are," said Eddie, and he snatched the carrot and gave it to Flame.

Sam turned red with rage.

"Get this straight. This pony is *mine* and I can do what I like with it. Ride it, hit it, shout at it, whatever, and you are just a little nobody who can't hack it!" she said, and turned on her heels.

Moments later the Mercedes roared out of the farmyard. Farmer Draper came and stood in the doorway. He looked at Eddie and Eddie returned the look. In that moment he decided that whatever else happened, Flame was not going to go to Sam.

Chapter Eleven

THE TORMENT OF OLD CHEESY

That afternoon Mr Wensleydale was doing his rounds. He was just about to leave the ward with Kalim when someone said: "How ya doin', Cheesy?"

Mr Wensleydale looked at Kalim. It obviously wasn't her. She wouldn't dare. Then who? There *were* only the patients there. Mr Wensleydale narrowed his eyes. He looked around the ward, then down at Emma and Hannibal, who often accompanied him on his rounds, then at Kalim.

"Did you hear that?" he asked.

"Hear what?" asked Kalim, trying not to smile.

"That voice, insulting me."

"I . . . yes, I did, Mr Wensleydale," said Kalim.

"Ever change your socks, Cheesy? WHOOO!" said the voice.

"There it is again!" said Mr Wensleydale.

He began to realise the awful truth. He approached Nelson. He glared at the parrot and Nelson glared back. Nelson liked staring competitions and had never lost one yet. Mr Wensleydale turned away.

"Bothersome little tyke! Irksome *bête noire*!" said Nelson.

"I have given my whole life to the welfare of animals and wildlife, and what do they do? This!" said Mr Wensleydale.

"Put a sock in it, Cheesy!" said Nelson, then screeched with laughter.

"Who taught this bird these things?" asked Mr Wensleydale.

"I don't know," said Kalim. "Maybe he just . . . picked them up."

"Pah!" said Mr Wensleydale, and left the ward.

"Bye bye, pretty boy! Bye bye, Cheesy!" shouted Nelson after him.

Mr Wensleydale slammed his office door, and alone in his room he was left to dwell on the fact that Nelson's owner wouldn't be collecting him for another two weeks. He wasn't sure he could bear a fortnight of insults and screeching laughter. He had a fairly good idea who had taught Nelson, but proving it would be difficult.

Kate telephoned the Country Park and spoke to the manager, who said yes, in principle, they would be very interested in acquiring another pony. He would have to see Flame first and have her checked over medically, but if she was in sound health there was a good chance the Country Park would take her, especially as she would, as Kate assured him, be coming for free.

Kate went to meet Eddie at the animal hospital to tell him the good news. Eddie had just returned from walking Emma in the park and he told Kate about his encounter with Sam at

Meadow Farm.

"I mean, it's useless," he said. "With the money from local businesses, we've now got four hundred and ten quid, which is brilliant, but not brilliant enough. And Greg is selling a few things to help, but that probably won't add up to much, so we're stuck, even if the Country Park will take her."

"Don't be such a dink," she said. "There's always a way to make things happen."

"You tell me what it is then," said Eddie.

"I don't know yet, do I? Maybe we could go and beat this Sam kid up," she said.

"Not your most subtle idea, Kate," said Eddie.

However, the days came and went and

neither of them could think of a way of keeping Flame. Eddie offered Farmer Draper the money they did have but he told Eddie that business was business and Flame would be sold on Saturday.

Eddie thought of staying away, but in the end he felt he owed it to Flame herself to be there with her on her last day at Meadow Farm. He took her for a final walk and gave her an apple, then sat on the fence stroking her head. She nuzzled him and showed him her skipping little run which she had become so proud of. She was quite fast and could keep exercising for hours. She was going to be a strong pony.

"I'm going to miss you, girl," said Eddie

The Mercedes cruised into the yard, a small horse box hooked behind it. Sam and her father got out of the car. Sam approached Eddie and took the rope he used to lead Flame from him. She slipped the rope off Flame's neck and threw it in the mud.

"Now she's mine, she won't have to wear old tat any more," she said smugly, taking from her pocket a red leather lead rein with JASMINE in gold letters on it.

"Her name's Flame," said Eddie.

"Not any more," said Sam. "Come on, Jasmine."

She tried to put the new lead over Flame's ears, but the foal tossed her head and backed away.

"Here! Come here!" shouted Sam.

Flame backed further away. Sam became furious.

"Stupid thing!" she said.

Farmer Draper shouted to Eddie, "Bring her in, boy."

Much against his will, Eddie went to Flame and, with a few soothing words and a light touch, led her into the horse box. Moments later Eddie stood and watched as the Mercedes left the yard. Flame could just see over the door of the box and she watched Eddie as she left the only home she had ever known. Then she was gone.

Eddie collected his bike and, with a last look at the paddock, he left. There was no point in hanging around now. He would probably never see Flame again.

Chapter Twelve

AN EMERGENCY

It was a week after Flame had gone and Eddie was at the hospital. He was doing his usual chores after school: feeding and walking Emma; feeding Hannibal; helping clean and feed the patients. Nelson was due to be collected and it wasn't a moment too soon for Mr

Wensleydale. Nelson had tormented him all week. He was just giving the parrot a check over before he left.

"The wing is fine now. And so it should be, considering how long he's been here," said Mr Wensleydale.

"Put a sock in it, Cheesebreath," said Nelson.

"Someone should put a sock in your beak," said Mr Wensleydale.

"Bothersome little tyke! Irksome *bête noire*!" said Nelson.

Eddie giggled and Mr Wensleydale shot him an accusing look. He knew it was Eddie who had taught Nelson the insults, but how could he prove it? He was about to say something when Chelsea entered.

"We've just had a phone call to say a pony has escaped from a private field and ran across a motorway. The police are trying to find her and they want us on hand. Hilary and Ron are about to leave in the ambulance," she said.

"Right. Keep me informed," said Mr Wensleydale.

"What was the pony's name?" asked Eddie.

"At first I thought it might be the pony you looked after, Eds. Flame. But it can't be. This pony's name is Jasmine," said Chelsea.

And Eddie was gone.

Ron peered through the windscreen of the ambulance and put his foot down. They sped along roads, over the viaduct which crossed the motorway and screeched to a halt in a country lane beside a police car. Ron opened the window and a young policeman leant in.

"Hello there. The pony was seen about fifteen minutes ago crossing this field, then she disappeared in the woods over there. We've looked but she's gone, so it's just a question of cruising around and hope we get lucky. She almost got crushed on the motorway," he said.

"She must be terrified," said Eddie.

"Let's have a drive around and see if we can spot her," said Ron.

He started the van and they drove off, promising to keep in touch with the police on mobile phones.

"Stop the van!" Eddie said suddenly.

Ron jammed on the brakes.

"What is it?" asked Hilary.

"I know where she's headed," said Eddie.

"Where?" asked Hilary.

"Meadow Farm. Life wasn't great there but it was the only home she knew, and me and the others were there," he said.

"But how would she know the way there?" asked Ron.

"'Cos she's clever," said Eddie. "Come on, let's get a move on."

Ron started up again and drove through the lanes towards Meadow Farm. To get to the farm Flame would probably try to head across country Eddie thought, but most of the land was hedged and they could see that some fields were impossible to escape from. That meant she'd have to leave the fields and travel along the lanes and through the local town of Birchington. They decided to head for there; it was only a few minutes away.

Eddie started to chew his nails, a habit he thought he'd grown out of. As they approached the town he began to wonder if he was right. Perhaps Flame had just got lost, or injured, or run over. Perhaps . . . he gripped the dashboard as they drove into the main street.

There she was, with her distinctive skipping run, sweat pouring from her coat, going straight down the High Street. People were stopping to stare and most cars had slowed down. A window cleaner's van suddenly turned out of a side street and, as Flame veered across the road, terrified and confused by all this unaccustomed noise, it accelerated.

Eddie shouted, "No!"

Unable to watch, he closed his eyes and his heart sank as he heard a sickening crash.

Chapter Thirteen

DAZED AND CONFUSED

When he opened his eyes Eddie expected to see Flame lying on the road. Instead he saw the window cleaner's van crumpled against a parked car. The driver had swerved to miss Flame and crashed into a stationary vehicle. The driver got out, and apart from looking a bit dazed, was none the worse for wear. Flame had stood petrified, her chest heaving, but now she started to run again. Eddie jumped down from the ambulance and ran after her.

In her confusion Flame ran into the open doors of a supermarket. The shoppers looked startled and one woman screamed. Flame skidded on the floor and backed into a shelf. Two assistants gave chase. Eddie ran in and followed.

"Don't frighten her! Keep the noise down!" he hissed.

"Is it yours?" asked a woman.

"No, but she knows me. Let me get close and the rest of you back off."

Eddie approached quietly. Flame had foam and spittle around her mouth and nose, and her eyes were wild with fear. She was snorting and breathing heavily.

Her coat gleamed with sweat. Eddie stepped forward slowly.

"Flame, it's me, Eddie. Good girl. What's happened, Flame? You've had a real adventure, haven't you? Good girl."

Talking all the time he got closer and closer until he touched her muzzle. She looked at him and the fear within her subsided. He stroked her head, whispering all the time.

Hilary and Ron came in and approached them. Ten minutes later the three of them led Flame outside. Ron had telephoned for a horse box and Eddie led her into it, staying with her on the short journey to a local farm which Hilary knew. The farmer, a different sort from Farmer Draper, was all smiles and let them use a spare barn to check that Flame was all right. He also said she could stay overnight.

"No real damage done," said Hilary.

She decided against giving her a sedative, realising that Flame had exhausted herself so much that nature would soon take over. Within half an hour the pony was fast asleep in the straw. Eddie sat with her. He watched as the familiar blue Mercedes entered the farm, trailing a horse box. Dicky and Sam entered the barn.

"Can she be moved?" asked Dicky.

"Of course not. She's asleep," said Hilary.

"I'd like to take her back as soon as possible," said Dicky.

"I don't think you'll be doing that," said Hilary.

Eddie looked at her. What did she mean?

"What are you talking about? She's

my daughter's pony," said Dicky.

"She escaped," said Ron.

"An accident," said Sam.

"Negligence, I'd call it," said Ron.

"You showed yourself to be an irresponsible owner: the pony was almost involved in a serious accident; damage has been caused to two motor vehicles, the owners of which may decide to sue you. I personally shall take this to court, if necessary, and recommend that you are not allowed to own a pony for at least two years," said Hilary.

"Did you say they might sue me?" asked Dicky.

Hilary had hit him where it hurt most – in his wallet.

"Quite likely," said Hilary.

"Can't you put in a good word?" asked Dicky.

"I'll tell the truth, but I'm certainly not happy about returning the pony to your care," said Hilary.

"What about my six hundred and fifty quid?" he asked.

"I'll give you that," said Eddie rashly.

"By tonight?" asked Dicky suspiciously.

"Yes," said Eddie.

"Dad! Jasmine's my pony!" said Sam.

"Shut up and get in the car," said Dicky.

"And her name is Flame. That's what I've put on her medical card," said Hilary.

Dicky looked at Eddie.

"Bring the money to my place this evening and she's yours. You can have all the papers then," he said, and walked back to his car.

Ron and Hilary turned to Eddie.

"Did you really raise six hundred and

fifty pounds?" asked Hilary.

"And where are you going to keep Flame?" asked Ron.

"Don't worry, it's all in hand," said Eddie.

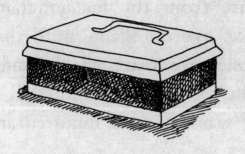

Chapter Fourteen

A Lot of Loose Ends

The first thing to sort out was the money. Eddie had been keeping all the money they raised in one of the lockers at the animal hospital. He knew it was stupid, and he kept meaning to put it in the Post Office, but he just hadn't done it. When they arrived back at the hospital, with a promise from the farmer that he'd keep an eye on Flame until the next day, Eddie went to the locker and took out the money. He counted it again. There was still four hundred and ten pounds.

He went to find Greg but he'd already gone home. He went back to the rest room and tried Greg's locker. It was open. Inside was a sweaty T-shirt, a photograph of Chelsea looking all lovey-dovey gooey eyed, a stained mug and a cash box. It was locked, of course. He went to the small cloakroom and there, in Greg's white coat, was a set of keys. Eddie took them and tried a likely looking one. Yes! he thought, as the cash box opened and inside he found three hundred pounds. Excellent. Eddie knew the money was for Flame, so he felt sure Greg wouldn't mind him taking it without his knowing, especially as it was an emergency. He took two hundred and forty pounds and put the rest back.

At six o'clock Eddie cycled up the drive of Dicky's house, paid the money and took a receipt, plus the papers detailing Flame's birth, weight, colour and ownership. As he cycled home he felt a twinge, imagining all the things he could have bought with that dosh: several new bikes; a computer; a CD player and loads of CDs; clothes; a telly and stereo. Oh well, he thought. What he hadn't got he wouldn't miss. And at last Flame was safe.

The next day Hilary contacted the

manager from the Country Park, who went straight to the farm where he met Hilary and Flame. By the end of the morning Flame had a new home, was making new friends and having a great deal of fun. Given that Eddie and his friends had raised the money, they would remain owners and have visiting rights whenever they wished. Now Eddie had two pets, Emma and Flame, neither of which lived in his home. He thought with regret how it should have been three – but his rabbit, Thumper, had died while still young.

After school Eddie went straight to the hospital. Chelsea congratulated him on saving Flame. Then he went to feed Emma and Hannibal. Greg was in the ward and beckoned to Eddie.

"Can you keep a secret?" he asked.

"Sure," said Eddie.

"It's about me and Chelsea. I promised her this posh engagement party with a string quartet and everything and I've been able to raise a few hundred pounds, but not enough. Do you think you could sort of, just hint to her, that we might have a . . . smaller party?"

"Me?" asked Eddie, flattered that Greg wanted him to intervene. "Sure, but . . ." And then the penny dropped. He realised with a slow cold horror what might have happened.

"This money . . . do you keep it in your locker?"

"Yes. Why?" asked Greg.

Eddie swallowed hard. There was no getting out of this one.

"Er, congratulations, Greg. You've

just become part owner of a pony."

Greg's jaw dropped and his face blanched. He reached forward and grabbed Eddie by the lapels. Greg wasn't a violent man but at that moment the thought of whacking Eddie Wright was very tempting. Then a sound made him turn, and there in the doorway, was Chelsea. She was laughing. She had heard everything and thought it was hilarious. Greg felt a mixture of relief and annoyance. Eddie started grinning too, until Chelsea stopped laughing and approached him.

"I can laugh, but that doesn't mean you can, Eddie. What do you think Mum and Dad will say when I tell them you pinched money from Greg?" she asked.

"Er, I s'pose they might be almost as

annoyed as they would be if they knew that you and Greg had watched that video the other night when they'd gone to bed. What was it called? *The French Maid and the . . .*"

"All right! All right!" said Chelsea, blushing slightly.

Greg was red in the face too.

"So – I'm off the hook, and so are you. A deal?" asked Eddie.

"A deal," said Chelsea reluctantly.

That Saturday, Hilary arranged a party at the hospital for Greg and Chelsea. Mr Wensleydale was so pleased that Nelson had now gone that he even allowed the drinks and crisps to be bought with money from the staff social fund. And, as usual, Kate had a brilliant idea. The dreadful Deidre and her fellow string players from the

school orchestra came and performed, so Chelsea got her string quartet after all.

And thanks to Eddie and his friends, Flame got a good home, Farmer Draper got his money and Sam . . . hopefully learnt that a pet is for life *only* if you look after it properly.

It was September and Charlie the tortoise was preparing for her long winter hibernation.

Eddie Wright sometimes wished he could hibernate too, especially when there was a test at school, or he'd got into some sort of trouble and had to face his parents when he got home. If you hibernated for six months, the world would seem completely new and fresh when you woke up.

Eddie had first got to know Charlie when she'd needed X-rays to examine a growth. She was brought into Rainbow Animal Hospital by her elderly owners, Mr and Mrs Dobson. When Charlie had returned home, Eddie used to call on the Dobsons to see her. He also did a few odd jobs for the couple. That morning he'd been helping them build a pond in their garden. They had put in the plastic lining, plants and water, but now they needed to let it settle for a few weeks before they could put the fish in.

Before Eddie left the Dobsons to visit the hospital, he tickled Charlie under her chin. He loved looking at the perfect formation of rings on the segments of her shell. He tried to tempt her with a bit of tomato, but she wasn't hungry. She was just beginning to get drowsy. As her metabolism slowed down ready for her hibernation, so did her appetite. Eddie wondered if tortoises had a sense of time, the way people did. Or perhaps when Charlie woke up in the spring, it would just seem like it was the next day.

"Have a good kip, Charlie," he said, and put her back in her wooden hutch. In a few weeks, when she was deeply asleep, she would be put in the garage and covered with straw. Eddie left her and cycled to the hospital.

Entering the hospital was like going home to Eddie. He loved it: the smells; the routines; the unexpected. He went through the double doors and smiled a 'hello' to his sister Chelsea, who worked in Reception. There were no patients and owners, so it was unusually quiet. Passing the familiar posters and photographs on the wall, Eddie went down the corridor to see Emma, the dog who lived at the hospital but whom everyone, even the grumpy chief vet, Mr Wensleydale, acknowledged as belonging to him. Emma came bounding across one of the wards as Eddie entered, licked him and wriggled like an eel with pleasure. Trundling behind her came Hannibal, an old bulldog, in a chariot which compensated for his crushed back legs. Eddie hugged him, smelling the rich doggy warmth of his fur, and the slightly less attractive, but no less loved, pong of his breath.

Then Eddie checked on some of the current patients: a squirrel with a broken leg, whose black eyes glittered through the cage at him; a cat with a cut paw; and a hedgehog who had got trapped in a lawnmower and almost starved because she couldn't get out. A few more decent meals of grubs and worms, another vitamin boost, and she would be set free. Eddie changed the bedding for the cat and fed Hannibal and Emma. Hannibal had to be restrained sometimes from helping Emma to finish her dinner too.

His chores done, Eddie went to say hello to Ron in the rest room. Ron, the ambulance driver, had his feet up and was sipping from a large mug that was so cracked and stained that no one else would use it. With his tea, he was nibbling a digestive biscuit. The biscuits were kept in a tupperware container and were meant to be for everyone. What happened, though, was that everyone else bought the biscuits, but only Ron ate them. He was extremely possessive about the biscuits and counted them every morning to make sure no one else had taken any. Eddie didn't bother to ask for one, because he knew the answer would be 'No'.

"Busy as usual, I see," Eddie said sarcastically.

"Been on duty since seven. No lunch break. This is the first time I've been able to have a cuppa and a nibble, so do me a favour and buzz off," said Ron.

Eddie was happy to 'buzz off' because he had heard voices in Reception, and voices probably meant a new animal. Eddie was gone before Ron could even grumble about what was wrong with young people today.

In Reception, a woman with wispy grey hair held a shoe box. Both she and Chelsea were peering into it.

"I tell you what, he's a lively little so-and-so," said the woman. "Look at that. Almost nibbled his way out. I reckon he was Houdini in another life, don't you?"

Eddie looked inside the box. An inquisitive, unafraid, small dark eye stared back at him. The other eye was closed. It was a pale-brown hamster, whiskers twitching, up on his back feet, front paws held in front of him, nose quivering – Eddie took in all the detail in a flash.

"Only got one eye but he don't miss a

trick. Know where I found him?" asked the woman.

Eddie shook his head.

"In me crunchy nut cornflakes. Right inside the packet, bold as brass and finished most of 'em an' all, I can tell you. Cheeky little so-and-so."

"So he's not yours?" asked Chelsea.

"No. Just turned up uninvited. Must have escaped from somewhere," said the woman, whose name was Martha Weston.

Eddie took the hamster from the box. He was careful to hold him with a hand cupped underneath, so as not to squash or frighten him. That way he would also avoid the possibility of getting nipped. The little creature stood up in Eddie's hand. He's used to being handled, Eddie thought.

Suddenly, the hamster ran up Eddie's arm, slid down his bomber jacket and landed in the pocket. Seconds later a hamster head popped out. He was holding a peanut which he had found there and started nibbling his prize. This was one clever animal.

Already Eddie could feel the familiar questions forming in his mind. What was his story? How did he come to be in Martha's house? To whom did he belong? If anyone was going to find out, it would be Eddie Wright.